➤➤ The Players ◄◄

Hungry Fox

Plump Goose

Baby Geese

———

For Norton Juster—you get the idea

Library of Congress Cataloging-in-Publication Data is available.
ISBN 978-0-06-220309-0
The illustrations for this book were rendered in pencil and watercolor with additional digital color and compositing.
Typography by Martha Rago.
13 14 15 16 17   SCP   10 9 8 7 6 5 4 3 2 1
❖
First Edition

Mo Willems

Presents

That Is NOT
a Good Idea!

Balzer + Bray

An Imprint of HarperCollins*Publishers*

"What luck!"

"Dinner!"

"Excuse me.

Would you care

to go

for a stroll?"

"Hmm . . .

sure!"

"That is NOT a good idea!"

"Would you care

to continue our walk

into the deep,

dark woods?"

"Sounds fun!"

"That is REALLY NOT a good idea!"

"Would you care

to visit my nearby

kitchen?"

"I would love to!"

"That is
REALLY,
REALLY
NOT
a good idea!"

"Would you care

to boil some water

for soup?"

"Certainly.

I do love soup!"

"That is
**REALLY,
REALLY,
REALLY
NOT**
a good idea!"

"Would you care

to look at my soup?

A key ingredient

is missing."

"That is REALLY, REALLY, REALLY, *REALLY* NOT a good idea!"

"Oh—

a key ingredient

IS missing."

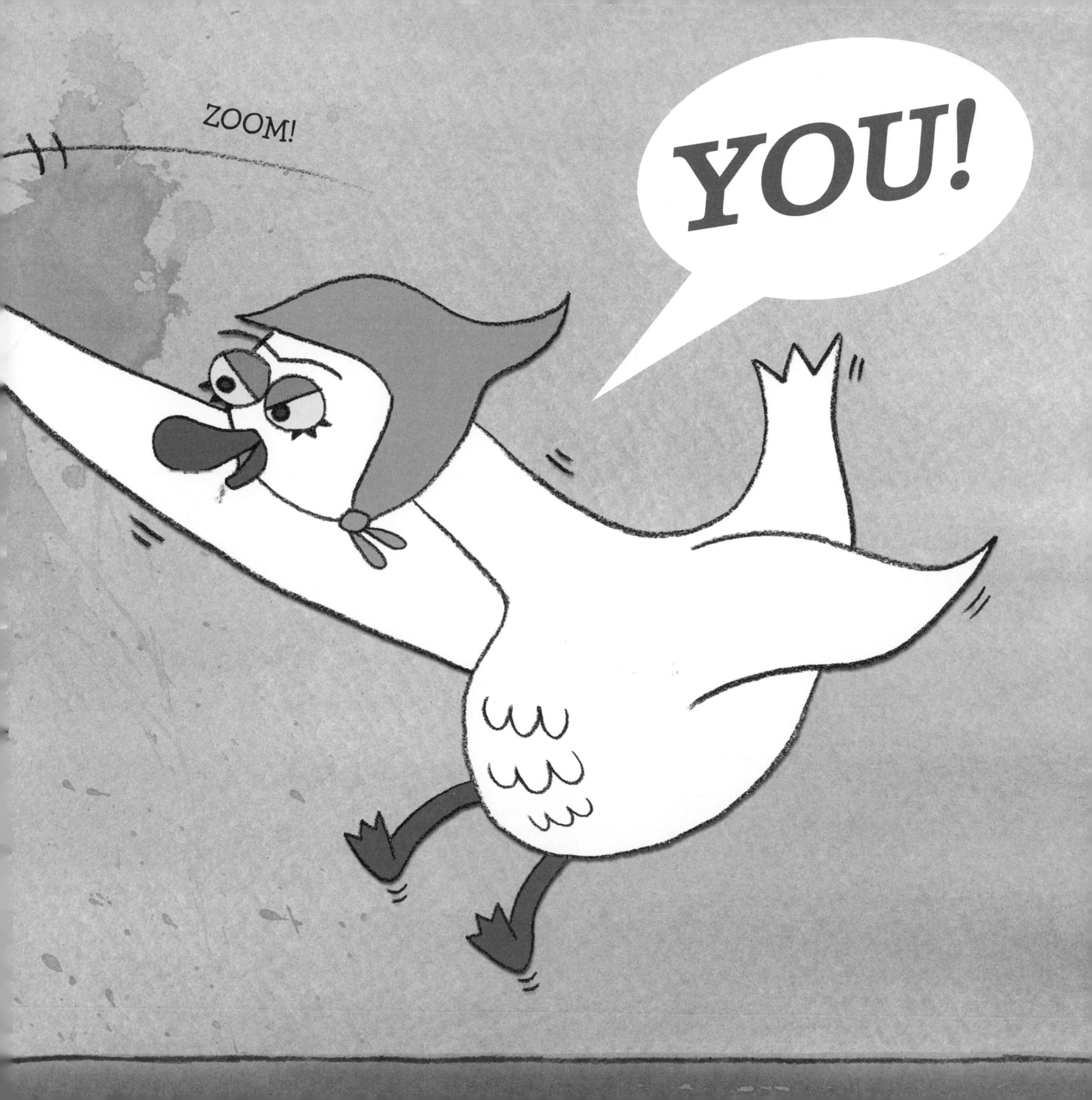
ZOOM!
YOU!

The END.